Pet Fairies to the Rescue!

Katie
the Kitten Fairy

Bella
the Bunny Fairy

The Pet Fairies

Georgia
the Guinea Pig Fairy

Lauren
the Puppy
Fairy

Harriet
the Hamster
Fairy

Penny
the Pony Fairy

Molly
the Goldfish
Fairy

ISBN 978-0-545-46295-2

10 9 8 7 6 5 4 3 2   12 13 14 15 16 17/0

Printed in the U.S.A.   40
First printing, November 2012

Pet Fairies to the Rescue!

by Daisy Meadows

SCHOLASTIC INC.

Spring has sprung!
The Pet Fairies and their pets are
thrilled.

The weather is beautiful, and there is so much to do!

Bella cleans her bunny's pen.
Molly and Harriet hang up the laundry.

Penny washes her pony's winter blanket.
"It's too warm for a blanket now!" she says.

Georgia, Katie, and Lauren are done with their chores.
They want to ride in the royal hot air balloon.

"It's the perfect day for it," Lauren says.

Georgia sees something come over the hill.
"It's Sparky, my guinea pig! Shimmer the
kitten and Sunny the puppy are with him,"
she says.

"Where have you all been?" Katie asks.
Sparky squeaks and runs in circles.
Sunny jumps.
Shimmer points.

"You are so silly," Georgia says with a laugh.
The hot air balloon sets down.
"It's our turn," Katie says.

All of a sudden, Sparky jumps up.
He grabs Georgia's wand in his teeth.

"Sparky!" Georgia yells.

The guinea pig takes off over the hill.

The puppy and kitten follow behind him.
"Our animals are trying to tell us something.
They must need our help," Georgia says.

The three fairies fly after their animals.
"Look, they're going into the Fairyland
palace," Katie says.

Sparky disappears through a tiny doorway.

"The door is so small," Lauren worries.

"We should follow them," Katie says.

Katie waves her wand, and the three fairies shrink.

"Now we will fit," Katie declares.

They all scamper through the small door. "Whoever lives here must be tiny," Lauren says.

"Look—there's Sparky," Georgia says.
Sparky waves his paw.

The fairies follow Sparky into a courtyard.
A family of mice is there.
They are all looking up.
The fairies join them.

"Oh, no!" Lauren cries.

Far above, there is a tiny, scared mouse.

He is on a high branch of a tall lilac tree.

"Miles climbed up," says the mama mouse,
"and he can't get down."

"We can help," Georgia says.

She nods to Sparky.

The guinea pig gives Georgia her wand.

Georgia recites a spell.

"With a fire for heat, the air will rise
And carry you back down from the skies.
But don't you fret or float away.
Return to safe ground, please don't delay."

There is a burst of sparkles,
and a hot air balloon appears.
It rises up to the tree.

Miles hops inside, and the balloon drifts down.

Miles looks over the edge of the basket, and he jumps.

The tiny mouse lands safely in his mother's arms.

"Oh, thank you," Papa Mouse exclaims.

The family gives Miles a big hug.
"We should all thank Sparky, Shimmer, and
Sunny," Georgia says.
She gives her guinea pig a good pat.

The fairies say good-bye to the mouse family.
Outside, Katie changes everyone back to
their normal size.

As they leave the palace, Sparky steals
Georgia's wand again.
"Oh, no! Where's he going now?" Georgia
wonders.

The fairies chase Sparky over a hill.
Sparky has climbed into the balloon!
"Follow Sparky, everyone!" Georgia calls.
"It's our turn for a balloon ride!"